The Kangaroo who couldn't HOP

Robert Cox & Jim Robins

Lothian
BOOKS

Thomas C. Lothian Pty Ltd
132 Albert Road, South Melbourne, Victoria 3205
www.lothian.com.au

Text copyright © Robert Cox 2001
Illustrations copyright © James Robins 2001
First published 2001
This paperback edition first published 2004
Reprinted 2005

National Library of Australia
Cataloguing-in-Publication data:

Cox, Robert.
    The kangaroo who couldn't hop.
    ISBN 0 7344 0717 3.

    1.Kangaroos - Juvenile fiction. I. Robins, Jim. II. Title.
823.914

Designed by Jo Waite Design
Colour separations by Eray Scan, Singapore
Printed in China by SNP Leefung Printers Limited

Out in the bush it was a big day for young kangaroos.

It was a day that only happened once every four years, the day when all young kangaroos were taken by their mothers to meet the leader of kangaroos in Australia.

His name was Big Red.

Mrs Grey lined up her four new children:
Jumper, Thumper, Bumper … and Keith.

Keith was the youngest. Mrs Grey looked at him sadly.

'Poor Keith,' she sighed. 'Whatever will Big Red say?'

The next day they all sat very still in front of Big Red: Mrs Grey, then Jumper, then Thumper, then Bumper and then … Keith.

Big Red looked up and smiled. 'Nice children, Mrs Grey. What do you call them?'

'Kangaroos,' replied Mrs Grey, who was rather nervous.

'No, no, no! Names, names, names!' boomed Big Red.

'Oh,' Mrs Grey felt silly.

'Well, this one is Jumper,' she said proudly.

Big Red nodded.

'… and *this* one is Thumper …' she said, doubly proud.

Big Red smiled.

'… and *this* one along here is Bumper …' she said, triply proud.

Big Red beamed.

'… and this one is … um … Keith.'

Big Red put his head on one side.

'Keith?' he said.

'Keith,' repeated Mrs Grey quietly.

Big Red shook his head. 'No, no, no! *Keith* is not a kangaroo's name.'

Mrs Grey looked along at Keith, who was staring at the ground. 'It was between Hoppy and … er … Keith,' she murmured. 'We chose Keith, Mr Grey and I.'

Big Red's eyes opened wide and he smiled broadly.

'Hoppy's a good name!' he exclaimed. 'Change it to Hoppy!'

Mrs Grey bit her lip and played with her lace handkerchief. 'But he *can't*,' she muttered.

'Can't what?' enquired Big Red, frowning.

Mrs Grey fiddled with her pouch and shuffled a bit. 'Can't hop,' she mumbled. 'He just can't *hop*! Poor thing. He's quite *hopless*!'

And, running to Keith, she flung her arms around his neck and burst into tears.

Big Red put an arm around her shoulder. 'Come, come, Mrs Grey,' he said kindly. 'We'll soon have Keith hopping. He's probably just a slow learner. *All* kangaroos can hop. You'll see.'

Mrs Grey shook her head sadly. 'No. We've tried everything, Mr Grey and I, but it's no good. Poor Keith … he's absolutely hopeless!'

'Come with me,' said Big Red.

So Mrs Grey, Jumper, Thumper and Bumper all hopped along behind Big Red. Keith walked.

Big Red stopped and watched as Keith plodded past him. Then he nodded.

'Ah yes!' he exclaimed. 'I see the problem. No *spring* in his heels.'

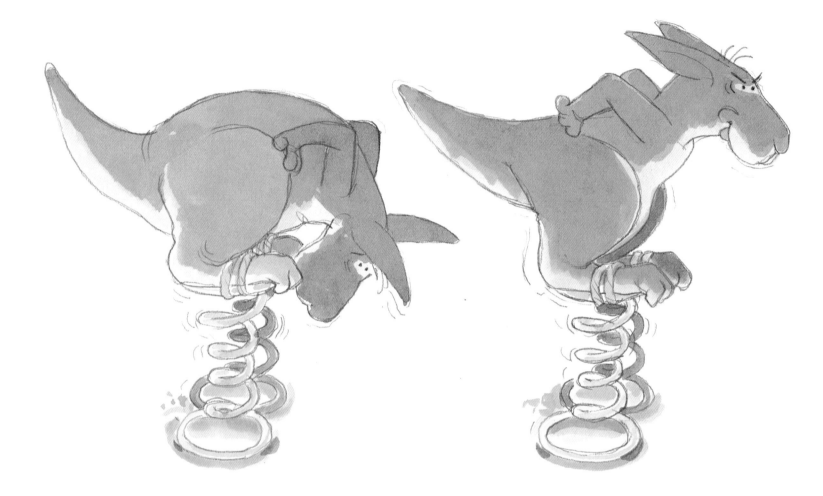

He went off and came back with two old bed springs, which he tied firmly onto Keith's large back feet with string.

'This'll do the trick,' he said. 'Go on, Keith! Hop!'

Mrs Grey, Jumper, Thumper and Bumper all crossed their fingers.

Keith closed his eyes, gritted his teeth, clenched his paws and went, 'N-n-n-n-n-n-g-g-g-g-g-g-h-h-h-h-h-h!'

Boing! Thud! Keith fell flat on his face.

Big Red shook his head. 'Right, it's got to be feathers. Is he ticklish?'

'Yes, very,' Mrs Grey replied. Jumper, Thumper and Bumper all giggled.

Big Red went away and came back with five fresh emu feathers. In the distance they could see an emu running around in circles, clutching his bottom and shouting, 'Ouch-ouch-ouch-ouch-ouch!'

Big Red looked back at the emu. 'He was only *too* pleased to help,' he said.

He handed a feather each to Mrs Grey, Jumper, Thumper and Bumper. He kept the largest for himself.

'Right, Keith,' he said, 'bend over.'

Keith bent over and they all tickled him like mad with their feathers.

Once again, Keith closed his eyes, gritted his teeth, clenched his paws and went, 'N-n-n-n-n-g-g-g-g-g-h-h-h-h-h-h!'

And fell over again.

'He's fallen on my feather,' said Jumper.

'And mine,' moaned Thumper.

'He's snapped *mine* in two!' cried Bumper, looking sadly down at his limp feather.

'Poor Keith,' said Mrs Grey with a tear in her eye. 'He'll *always* be hopeless!'

Big Red shook his big red head. 'Does he like the heat?' he asked.

'Hates it!' said Mrs Grey. 'You'll always find him in the shade.'

'Good,' said Big Red. 'Hot rock! That *always* cures slow hoppers.'

Mrs Grey looked very worried. 'Will it hurt him?'

Big Red grinned at her. 'Not if he hops off quickly enough! That's the whole idea. This one's got to work! Even humans hop off hot rock.'

He pointed to a flat rock, sizzling in the sun.

'Go on, Keith,' he ordered. 'Up on the rock you go!'

Mrs Grey, Jumper, Thumper and Bumper all turned away and covered their eyes.

Keith climbed onto the hot rock.

Then he closed his eyes, gritted his teeth,
clenched his paws and went,
'N-n-n-n-n-g-g-g-g-g-g-h-h-h-h-h-h!'

Thud! They all looked up at Big Red.
'Did he hop?' asked Mrs Grey excitedly.
'Fell,' said Big Red sadly. Then he
scratched his big red head and said, 'Come
with me, please.'

Mrs Grey, Jumper, Thumper, Bumper and
Keith all sat very still in front of Big Red as he
wrote on a large piece of paper.

'Here you are,' he said, handing the paper
to Mrs Grey. 'Your last chance. The
hop-spital. You'll see a Dr Leapyear. He'll
fix Keith up all right.'

Dr Leapyear was a hop-tician. He peered
into Keith's eyes. 'Hmmm,' he said, 'A
hopless case!'

Mrs Grey was quite upset. 'Yes, I know
that! That's *exactly* why we're here!'

'Hmm,' said Dr Leapyear again, frowning. 'Had one before, y'know. Very rare. Tail was too heavy. Absolutely hopeless!'

Mrs Grey's eyes widened and her mouth dropped open in astonishment.

'Tail too *heavy*!' she exclaimed. 'So what did you do?'

Dr Leapyear leaned forward and looked
at Keith over his glasses.
'WE CUT A BIT OFF!' he cried. 'AND
THAT'S WHAT WE'LL DO TO YOU!'

Keith suddenly leapt up in the air.

Boing! Boing! Boing! Boing! Boing! Boing! Boing! Boing!

The hopless kangaroo had finally found his hop!

He hopped around the room three times and then *right* out of the door.

BOING! BOING! BOING! BOING! BOING! BOING! BOING!

Mrs Grey jumped up and hugged the doctor. She was very affectionate.

'Would you really have cut a piece off his tail?' she asked.

Dr Leapyear looked at Mrs Grey, horrified. 'Good heavens, no!' he said. Then, with a wink, he added, 'But Keith didn't know that, did he, my dear?'

Mrs Grey smiled.

And Keith? Well, he just couldn't stop hopping!

BOING! BOING! BOING! BOING! BOING! BOING! BOING!